ALISTAIR'S TIME MACHINE

by Marilyn Sadler

Illustrated by Roger Bollen

M

MACMILLAN CHILDREN'S BOOKS

Alistair Grittle was a boy of science.

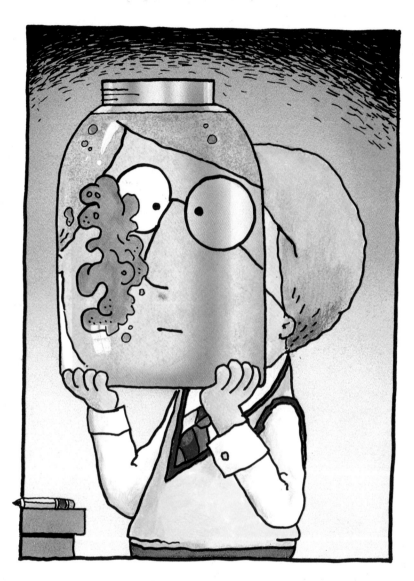

He collected slimy things in jars.

There was nothing he enjoyed more than watching cells divide.

And he knew the Milky Way like the back of his hand.

So one day when Alistair decided to enter Twickadilly's Second Annual Science competition, everyone was certain he would win first place.

Alistair considered many different projects before deciding
on a time machine.

The time machine was easier to build than Alistair expected.

When Alistair finished his time machine, he decided to test it.
He told his mother not to expect him for lunch.

Alistair did not want to go too far back in time. So he set his
time machine for the day before yesterday. Then he pushed
a button.

Alistair's time machine did not take him to the day before yesterday. It took him somewhat farther back in time.

Alistair had lunch with some knights at a round table.

After lunch Alistair decided to take his time machine home.
He was quite disappointed that it did not work.

But Alistair's time machine did not take him home.

It took him to a royal ball at a palace in France.

It took him out to sea on a pirate ship.

It took him to an arena in Rome.

It even took him to a campsite where some cave people were trying to start a fire.

Alistair was not in the mood to teach the cave people how to start a fire.

So he gave them some matches. Then he set out for home again.

Alistair was just about to travel through time, when all of a sudden some stampeding woolly mammoths came charging out of the brush.

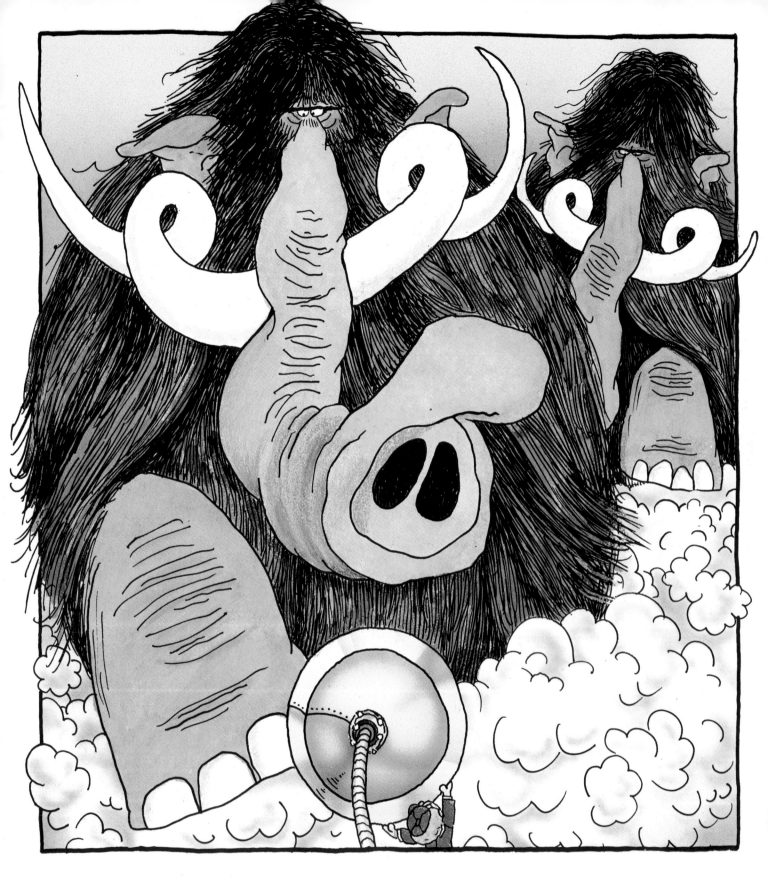

Alistair did not want the cave people to be trampled. So he turned his time machine on the woolly mammoths.

The woolly mammoths disappeared into time. Alistair hoped
he had not sent them to the palace in France.

The cave people had never seen anything like it. They asked Alistair to sit for some cave paintings.

Alistair said goodbye to the cave people. Then he tried once more to go home.

This time he was delighted to find himself back home in his basement. His time machine worked after all.

Alistair did not want to be late for the science competition.
So he left straight away.

Alistair could tell that the judges liked Hector Dowdy's model of the solar system. All of the planets turned around the sun, when Hector pushed a button.

The judges thought Alistair's time machine was quite clever.
But when Alistair pushed the button to take the judges
through time, nothing happened.

The judges did not think that Alistair's time machine worked.
So they gave the first place ribbon to Hector Dowdy.

Alistair thanked the judges for a most challenging science
competition. Then he left for home.

Alistair knew that his time machine worked . . .

. . . but how could he prove it?

First published in Great Britain 1986 by
Hamish Hamilton Children's Books

Picturemac edition published 1988 by
Macmillan Children's Books
A division of Macmillan Publishers Limited
London and Basingstoke
Associated companies throughout the world

Reprinted 1991

British Library Cataloguing in Publication Data
Sadler, Marilyn
Alistair's time machine.
I. Title   II. Bollen, Roger
823'.914[J]

ISBN 0-333-48088-0

Printed in Hong Kong